Senior Kane

by

Eddie J Martin

A woman can hold a grudge longer than any man, just asked any man.

Due to the variable conditions, materials, and individual skills, the publisher, author, editor, translator, transcriber, and/or designer disclaim any liability for loss or injury resulting from the use or interpretation of any information presented in this publication. No liability is assumed for damages resulting from the use of the information contained herein.

Show love to the living, the dead don't need it!

It's a bitch when you get old; you hurt where you never have before. Getting around isn't what it used to be, and women are very rare. Even when they're available things don't work like they used to, you need a lot of help or I might say at least some help.

Clients come by, but they seem to be looking for that young Ruben Kane. I still have the connections, may be more so that I've gotten older. Detective work is a young man's game not for the old, so now what I know will have to do. Maybe I should have been taking this route all the time, would have saved me a lot of knots upside the head.

Ruben Kane

Ruben Kane!

A bright skin negro in his early forties asked as he walked thru the office door. Average size, three-piece pin stripe blue suite, solid black tie, and white shirt, black studson shoes and Fedora on his head. Diamond rings on his fingers. His entire outfit must have hit him back at least a thousand dollars or more.

"Yeah, that's me, how can I help you?"

"Are you Ruben Kane? I thought you were a lot younger."

"You must be thinking about my son, they say we look-alike…

 No man, I 'm Ruben Kane, and there is no son. I'm all there is, now, how can I help you?"

He looked me up and down and saw a five foot ten, two hundred pounds dark skinned Sixty-two-year-old negro. hair graying but not yet bald, eyes had lost their glider but still had a glow. Two-inch scar down his left cheek:

"You know Mr. Kane, now that I see you, this may work out. I mean your age and all.

Okay, Mr. Kane, it's like this. Over at the nursing home, where my aunt is staying they've been having a lot of thefts, you may be just the person to stop it.

"I don't know Mr., what's your name again?"

Jonathan, Eric Jonathan. My father's name is Ralph Jonathan. He owns the city's Waste Treatment Plant. Yes, I think you may be just the man we're looking for.

Let's hear what you got, I said. Why don't she just move.

"You know old people Mr. Kane, i tried to persuade her to do just that but she won't do it, says she feel at home there.

We were thinking maybe you could lease a suite over there and just nose around, perhaps you could find out who is doing all the thievery."

"How long you giving me to locate the thief, and how much am I getting paid, and who's paying for the nursing home? We are talking about quite a bit of money you know? I charge two hundred up front plus fifty dollars a day."

"Don't you worry about the money Mr. Kane, I'm going in with some of the other relatives in the home, and we can handle it?" As far as how long it takes, we'll leave that up to you."

"Well, in that case, you got your man, when do I start?"

"We've got a suite reserved for you, and all you have to do is move in."

"One other thing does anyone know I'm coming besides you and the others?"

"No, we thought it would be better that way."

"That's good enough for me Mr. Jonathan, just leave me a deposit, and I'll get right on it."

Two days later I was walking through the doors of Mac Cleaver nursing home and shown to my suite. Fourth floor, suite 428. One bedroom, bath, living room, kitchen net and patio. The residents were all nationalities and ages, maybe that's the reason for the bland food. The ages were between 65 and 85, everyone looked like they function well and some of the old broads acted spry. There was a lounge room where **everyone went after dinner. Pool table, ping-pong table, darts, TV, etc. Sometimes I hear they even have dances.**

Welcome to the palace…

I turned toward the voice and found a little old man of the age of 68 speaking to me. Three-piece pinstripe suit with a bowtie. White shirt, gold watch. Rings, and the one on his pinky finger I didn't think was imitation diamond. Gold rim glasses, goatee, white eyebrows, and a head full of white hair. Light chocolate brown skin looks like he came from the islands or somewhere across the water.

"Come on over and have a seat, he said." Talk to me." I'm Jonas McIntyre, and your name is?

Ruben Kane, I said.

You call this place the palace, is that a name the residents call it?

You got that right, Jonas said. That's because there's so much money floating around here. Everyone here has either got money or their relatives has. That's the reason we've been having so many thefts lately. They haven't gotten to me yet, I'm too smart for um.

And what was your occupation Mr. Kane? Everyone that's in here is retired from something.

My previous employment, Ruben said. Was as a consultant, I did that for over 30 years and I thought it was time for me to give it up. See how the other side live.

Well Ruben you come to the right place or maybe not, depending on if you get robbed or not. We've had five thefts so far, watches, rings, and cash. They seem to know when a person is home or not. I think it's an inside job myself.

Have you noticed something Ruben? They have more women around here than men and they are the ones getting robbed the most. They leave their stuff all out in the open for everybody to see, and like I said since they've got the money or their relatives anyway they don't seem to give a damn. If you're going to be **a thief, this is the best place to be.**

I notice that some of the women here don't look bad, you ever think that some of them couldn't be doing the stealing. After all women do steal you know, and if the women here are the only ones that getting their jewelry stolen it could be by another woman.

You know, I never thought of that Ruben. You could be right. And they do have lovely women here and all dressed impeccably. But then that's what they do here, from the time they get up in the morning till the time they go to bed.

I know they don't stay around here 24 hours a day, what else do they do?

All I know, around noon you will find the place getting empty. You'll see more limousines around here then you ever seen especially on a Wednesday and Sunday. Kids coming to get their parents to take them shopping and lunch. Sometimes the kids aren't even in the car, just the chauffeurs, and stuff up the ass. Name of the company right on the side of the bag. And you know the next day down here in the lounge they must show it all off. Some have men friends they take with them and they come back loaded.

Do they have a lot of that going on?

More than you would think. I don't know what people think of seniors, but we have sex on average of three times a week, and if it was up to some of these women it would be more than that.

I notice that a few of the ladies have had their eyes on you since you walk through the door, better stock up on your Viagra, you will need that because you will copulate, the ladies will see to that. Unless you're gay that is, you're not gay are you Mr. Kane?

No, I'm not gay and I may be in Tice to indulge in a sexual encounter from time to time. Just lead me to it.

I'm glad of that because we men are outnumbered here and a few of these men, I'll have to tell you, I have to take up the slack for a few. So, for one I'm glad you here.

Over in the corner of the room I noticed a bar, who would have thought that you could find a bar in a nursing home. I didn't run just walked very fast in that direction. The bar wasn't very large just six stools, now if they just had my drink and they did. Jack Black, and I ordered a double.

The bartender was a small little old lady of about 68 and looked it. Silver hair which she was losing but had all her teeth dentures for sure. The one thing she did have was diamonds, a lot of diamonds. Since she could pour a drink she was all right with me. There were a few tables around the bar with 2 to 3 lounge chairs, mostly ladies sit there but an occasional man. They had all looked at me when I ordered a drank and I heard one lady say, "new meat"

Part 2

come over and sit with us, you don't have to be shy, what's your name?

Ruben Kane, I said as I move over to the table and sat my drink down. And who do I have the pleasure of addressing?

The one to my left, about 65 and light skin black woman. and still holding her own. Long fingers that held the diamonds and she made sure I saw them. My name is Eda she said. And I'm the party girl, do you like to party Mr. Kane?

Kind of gotten a little old for that Eda.

You're never too old Mr. Kane, there's always something that'll help your get-up and get it.

The one sitting right across from me was Italian (I think) and she was midsize and if I were to go by what I heard about Italian women, I'd say a good cook. That is if women with this much money cook for themselves. But the rings she had on…

And I'm Amy.

The one woman to the right of me with her legs crossed was a little older than the others and dare I say much cuter. You could tell she'd been taking care of herself, from head to toe. I found out later she had been Miss Ohio in her day. She carried herself well and if I had to use a Viagra or two I'd want to start with her.

My name is Ruby she said. She didn't have as many diamonds as the others but what she did have on was huge. All had on necklaces, diamonds. All looked money.

Are you all moved in Mr. Kane? Where did they put you? Ruby asked.

I am thank you, and I'm on the fourth floor, suite 428.

You are only a few doors down from me Eda said, we're neighbors. I'm at 419. We can do coffee some mornings.

20 minutes later I departed the ladies mentioning I would see them later. One of them said, I'm sure you will.

I walked around a little more seeing what I could see but I stuck to the bottom floors.

A large patio with people playing pinochle and sitting around the pool under umbrellas. A few was in the pool playing grab ass. I'll have to say these women are nothing like my old grandmother use to be seems like the rich are different.

One of the ladies was coming out the pool and said. You just arrive?

Yes, I said.

Welcome to the castle. Do you swim she said?

I haven't in a while, I said.

You must come and join us she said, it really gets nice around midnight. You see things that will blow your mind.

Why so late, I said?

That's when the old fuddy-duddies are in bed.

She said her name was Marlene, her ex-husband owns the Archers Clothing store before he died. She's here at the castle because she didn't want to stay at that large home alone. As you can see this is the place to be if you still like to party, and I like to party.

Well Marlene let me get to know the place some and I'll be sure to get back with you.

I moved on around the pool looking at the ladies, none-looked under 60 but damn if they didn't look good for that age. While I was watching them, a few were reading books and watching me under eyed.

I set down on a lounge chair and stretched out, it would have been nice if I had on some shorts. There was a waiter and I ordered a drink. Vodka tonic. It came with an umbrella on top and a slice of lime, not bad, the view was even better from where I was sitting.

She spotted me about the same time I spotted her, of course I notice her from the neck down first. Same long neck connected to shoulders that was military shaped and formed. Breasts still rounded and firm. She must be in her late 50s or early 60s now, but legs still in nice shape for the work she was into.

She and a friend of hers were in the business of prostitution, they call them SALT and PEPPER. One was black, and one was white I was looking at pepper the white one.

Ruben Kane, she said you do get around. How long has it been? Ten, fifteen years or more? How you been? You still look the same, life must be treating you good.

And you Pepper, you still look the same a little off the hips but that's all right. I thought you and Salt had left this town long ago.

We did Ruben, this town was getting a little slow for us and so we hit Miami for a few years and then Los Angeles. A few other places and finally ended up in

Alaska. We ran into Smooth up there and started working for him, best decision we ever made we earn a ton of money so could retire. Salt headed for California and I'm back here.

Now that's my story, what about you? You still doing that detective work?

Pepper I'm still into it, I'm on a case now. I was hired to find who ripping the place off. So, for now I'm on the down low, keep it quiet about what I do.

We've been hit several times pepper said. No one can catch the robbers. If you're that same old Ruben Kane I'm sure, you'll find them damn quick.

What are you doing here, you still kind of young to be in a place like this? I said.

Oh, didn't I tell you, I'm part owner in this place. I was never told that the children were going to hire someone, I'm glad it's you.

Can I call on you if I need your help?

Sure, you can Ruben, I got to go right now maybe I'll see you later.

You not still working are you pepper?

I keep my feet wet now and again to see if I still have it, you know how it is?

I watched pepper walk away, she had that same swing to her body that she had years ago, and I imagine she commanded near that same price. I had a chance once of laying up with her, but thing was the time never was right and my money wasn't right. As I recall neither one was given it up for free.

About ten years ago I ran across them in the old ebony club, I was on a case at that time looking for someone for a client. I walked over to their table and shot the usual shit with them. Salt asked me was there anything they could do for me and I replied it would be nice, but the price was too high. Pepper said to me, it just so happens Ruben today there is a discount.

I didn't know you girls gave discounts I said.

For you Ruben, salt said. we'll make on exception.

At that time, I spotted the person I was looking for, told the girls I must take a rain check.

I saw the girls off and on for the next few years, but I was always into something and we never got together. Maybe this time!

A few days later I decided to return to my office never know what I may have missed. As I walked through the door there was Rita. I hadn't seen her in some years, since she left my employment and got married. Rita had been with me a few years as my secretary we really went through sometimes together. Rita is 5'5 around 275 or was when she was with me, looks like she hasn't lost much. She used to carry a stiletto knife in her bosom and could use it. I saw her once go to work on a guy there in the office and it wasn't anything nice. She was a Mexican illegal that came over the border and I needed a secretary and she started working for me, after a while she met a fella and got married.

Rita, I said, haven't seen you in a while you decided to stop by and see old RK?

RK I've missed you too, I had a feeling you were in the same old location. Still paying the same old rent I'll bet?

You know I am Rita, you can't beat two-dollar rent. So, What's up Rita?

Well, I come to see if I could get my old job back, you don't have anyone do you?

I had somebody for a while, but I lost them like I did you, to marriage. By the way are you still married?

It's a long story RK but the short version is I caught my husband and some la – la in bed together and I started cutting on they ass. The judge gave me six months and I'm out on parole right now. The husband and I will be getting a divorce as soon as he gets out the hospital.

What happened to the girl?

Last I heard she was in the same room with a bed beside him. They can give each other blood transfusions as far as I'm concerned.

Sure, I said. You can have your old job back, everything is still there.

Oh yeah, I'm goanna need the rest of the day off.

Same old Rita I said. While you out pick me up a couple bottles of Jack Black.

Same old RK she said.

After Rita left to take care of whatever business she had to take care of I went to my desk and basically just look around to see what I had lingering. That last case of finding a divorcee paid me right at $1100 and took me four days. That'll go into one of my logbooks, Rita will take care of that from here on. All I have to do now is what I do best. Mail, I had to catch up on that, there is no sense having Rita start her first day with my old correspondence.

There was one letter that looked interesting.

Mr. Kane, I need your help in a situation I have, and I think you're a good man for the job. Would you please call me at this number, 441-6724? PS this job contain some danger.

The next day I headed back to the palace, I left a note for Rita telling her where I'd be and the number to my room. I learned that the past weekend one of the lady's suits got Rob and the police were called in this time. I was beginning to think that it was on inside job it seemed like the robbers only hit on the weekends. I decided this weekend I'd stay close.

Thursday was a hotter than usual in Cleveland and I remembered what one of the ladies said about midnight swim. I picked up a pair of swim trunks and eleven that night I proceeded to the pool. From what I was told I could have left my trunks back in the room but I'm not that bold. When I entered the pool area I saw a lot of skin, topless, bottomless and some both. The age I guess was from 58 on the up, a lot of these old broads had bodies that would put a teenager to shame. I walked around until I found a chase chair to sit on and I needed that by then my Boner was just about busting through my trunks and I almost fell into the pool watching the ladies. Once I sit down I still had to cover up with my hands until I found a book.. I'd say it was about 50 people in and around the pool mostly women. One woman I saw getting out the pool saw me watching her this was one of the ones with no top and about 62 years of age. She walked over to me and bending over me said. You knew around here aren't you, I've seen you around but never got to introduce myself. What's your name?

Ruben Kane, I said. What's yours?

Gloria Baker she said

you have nice breasts Gloria.

I'm glad you think so Ruben, but I bet you tell all the girls that.

Only the ones that have nice breasts I said.

Look I have a previous engagement right now can we get together later?

I'll be looking forward to it Gloria.

After Gloria left I heard a voice say "do I have nice breasts also?

I looked over to my left and there was a tall white lady looking over at me under one of Theos large floppy straw hats. I say tall lady because she was almost as long as the lounge chair she was laying on.

Pardon I said.

You were saying how nice Gloria's breasts were, I asked you about my breasts?

Do you know Gloria I said?

Everyone knows everyone in the palace but you I seem to have missed. I did hear you tell Gloria your name was Ruben Kane. My name is Sent.

My breasts? Ruben.

Part 3

I set up and took a good look at them. The nipples were small and red, the surrounding area were darker red. The size was melon shaped but too small for her body. Of course, I didn't tell her that, but I wouldn't think of kicking her out of bed.

Well, she said?

Nice I said. Very nice. Someday I'd like to get to know them.

Some day was later that night I didn't even need Viagra. If you ever wondered how a Python felt wrapped around you…That was it.

Before lunch that next morning I was back in my own place, it wasn't all sex, I did find out a few things. Sent said the thief had to be someone that lived there and no more than two.

There's probably been more people getting robbed then said, these women have more jewelry then they own up to but they're not saying. I really think they don't know how much stuff they have themselves.

At lunch I met up with Jonas McIntyre, He was sharp as usual. Three-piece pinstripe suit gold watch and diamond rings to match

what's going on Ruben? I heard you made the swim set the other night, Sent is nice, isn't she?

Nothing get past you does it Jonas?

Not much Ruben, not much. We sit there and shot the shit for 30 minutes and he said that he had a run to make.

I thought I'd call my broker, haven't call him in a couple of days, don't even know what that last number was I played, may have some bread waiting on me.

Bernie, Ruben Kane here. How's it hanging.

I was about to spend this little change I was holding for you Ruben, didn't think you wanted it.

How much you holding for me Bernie?

$275, you hit on number 258.

I'll tell you what Bernie, put it on number 275 and play it for the next three days. I'll call you back in the next few days I expect to be out of pocket for a while.

Oh yeah, Rita is back with me, so I have a secretary now.

That night I made it over to the ebony club, my old stomping grounds. I saw a couple of ladies I knew so I joined them. Joyce and Ruby were both workers and I had done a favor for them once. Like getting rid of their pump. who was beating up on them and they wanted some relief, I help them with that. They offered to buy me a drink and I accepted, it's not too often a hooker offered to buy you a drink.

As we talked I happen to spot Jonas sitting at the end of the bar talking to Jacob the bartender. What caught my attention was the item Jonas gave him? Not out in the open like you would hand someone something but underhanded and Jacob received it as such.

Now I know that Jacob was known to receive stolen goods, everyone has a hustle and his was stolen goods. I heard he made a good living at it, he been at it for ten years or more.

To be sure I asked the girls and they confirmed it. Jacob and Jonas went into a back room, ten minutes later they come out. Jonas got another drink and left.

I think I found my thief.

The guy that's leaving, I asked the girls. Do you know him? Does he come in here often? One of the girls said he comes in here about twice a month, stayed about an hour talking to Jacob. Go in the back and leave. I think he's into selling Jacob Jewelry. We even bought several pieces. I saw the same guy cross town at a pawn shop.

Well thanks ladies, could I buy you another?

Sure can Ruben, is there anything we can do for you?

Maybe later I said.

I think I should have a talk with Jonas, if I can I'll try to keep this from the law, I kind of like the old boy. Wouldn't want to see him go to jail especially at his age.

If there is more than him then all bets are off.

That next Saturday, 11 PM I met him in the hall and asked him was he going to lunch? I don't think so Ruben, I think I'll dine in town today. While I'm there think I'll pick up a few goods. I need a new sport coat, things like that. Hey, they're having a dance here tonight, your goanna make it?

Can't think of anything better I said.

After lunch I decided to take a walk, it wasn't that hot, and I needed the exercise.

As I was walking out the door I ran into a Pepper, told her where I was going, and she said watch yourself Ruben we still have some lowlife young men around here.

I'm too old to have my ass ripped off so I went back up to my room to fetch a little help.

Mr. McIntyre nice to see you again so soon.

Yeah Jeffrey I need me some summer rags.

I think we can help you out, our summer fashions just arrived. You can look around or we can have our models, model you something.

I'll tell you what Jeffrey, I don't feel much like walking I'll just go over here to the lounge and you can send a few people over with what you think I'd like.

Would you like your usual champagne?

Jeffrey, you know what I like.

An hour later Jonas walked out the clothing store with a couple of packages which had sport jacket, three summer shirts, socks silk pants and sandals. He hopped into a taxi

and was taking too an eatery, had the taxi wait for him while he ate and was taken back to the palace.

On the way back to the palace the taxi driver drove through the park. On the way Jonas spotted an ambulance and police cars and there was the attendant treating Ruben Kane. He'd have to ask Ruben about what happened when he gets back to the palace.

An hour later a police car dropped Ruben off at the palace, how's your head he asked?

I'll live I said.

You know you could have killed those two thugs, why didn't you?

I didn't want to kill the old boys, takes too much out of you.

Have you ever killed anyone before Mr. Kane?

Yes, Ruben said. I was in the military.

You do have a license for that derringer? The officer said.

Yes, I still have my license as a PI.

Okay Mr. Kane, if we need to get in touch with you can we reach you here?

I'll be right here officer.

Ruben got out the police car and walked slowly (very slowly) into the palace.

Gloria saw him coming in and said Ruben, baby, what happened?

You should see the other guy I said.

What happened Ruben?

Look, I don't feel so good I need to go to my room and lay down, I'll get with you later.

Back in his room he pulled out his derringer, wallet and keys and threw them on the table and dropped on the bed and closed his eyes. Then the phone rang.

RK this is Rita, wanted to let you know that a call came in about a case you promised to take. He says you never call him back.

I never said I'd take the case but nevertheless if he call's back tell him I'm about to wrap this case up and I'll give him a call. Anything else Rita.

 Well, your wife called, said that she would be going to her mother's for a few days and a fella exposed his self to me

How'd that go I said?

I told him to put that damn thing away before I cut it off, I think he got the message.

Part 4

At 11:30 I received a knock at my door, I didn't want to get up, but I did. It was Dorothy looking like a goddess, low-cut black dress off the shoulders, hair cut at the neck her inch-long **ear** rings and white necklace plus high heel shoes. (Looking good as she wants to)

Ruben aren't you coming to the dance she said. Everyone's there.

I guess you heard what happened to me today and I'm still not feeling up to it. I'll have to tell you as good as you look, make me want to come down to the dance anyway. Then I realized I had nothing on but my drawls. Come on in a minute while I put something on I said. I walked into the bathroom to wash up and the next thing I knew Dorothy was behind me kissing me on my neck. I turned around still in my drawls you understand and started kissing her back. I'm not that old that Junior didn't start standing at attention. While we were kissing, I raised her skirt and found she had no panties on. She grabbed me around the neck, I grabbed her around the butt. She put one foot on the sink, Junior came out of the split in my drawls and it was on. We both came at the same time and then both of us fail to the floor.

After Dorothy got herself together she went back down to the dance, I told her I would be along soon. After that episode with Dorothy I had to lay back down. After ten minutes I took a shower and got dressed. On my way out, I notice that I forgot my keys, while there I'd picked up the derringer, more by habit than anything. As I was coming out my room I saw Jonas entering a room that I knew wasn't his, he stayed on the next floor. He's at it again I thought. Shit changes and looked like it'll be the same for Jonas. I checked the derringer and slowly walked up to the door I saw Jonas go in. It was unlocked. He never noticed me, he was too busy looting the place and I shot him in the knee, someplace I knew he wouldn't walk away from. He screamed and drop to the floor and I close the door and continued down to the dance. On the way I passed a phonebooth and call the police. Informed them that there was a robbery in progress going on at that location. ten minutes later the police arrived and picked up Jonas and as you would have guessed he was the talk of the palace for the next week.

Breaking news

The palace Robber has been captured and is now in the county jail, sources says he was shot in the leg and police received an anonymous call. Yet it's not known who shot the robber and called in his location, but it is known that he was captured in the act of robbing one of the apartments of a resident.

Rita buzzed me on the intercom. RK, there is a Mr. Jonathan on the line.

Hello Mr. Jonathan?

I want to thank you for that job, you did a great piece of work. Didn't take long either.

The police never said who shot the robber, but I got the feeling it was you, am I right?

Could be Mr. Jonathan, I have a feeling that's the end to your troubles. Tell your aunt she can sleep easy tonight.

There is a check in the mail for you Mr. Kane and thanks again.

30 minutes later there was another call, it was pepper.

The girls miss you Ruben, you could have said goodbye.

I hate goodbyes I said.

When they caught that robber I kind of felt you had something to do with that, am I right?

Maybe, maybe not pepper.

Well, thanks anyway.

Oh yeah, Gloria asked about you, she said give her a call.

RK, Bernie's on the line.

Ruben, I'm tired of holding this money for you, you hit again.

I'll tell you what Bernie, I'll be right down.

(round two)

Round and around they went five kids, three white girls and two black boys. They were circling a doodad that was 8 feet high with little balls hanging down on rope, once the rope stopped the kids started going in the opposite direction. When the ball stopped then that person was out of the game; until the last and they were declared the winner. I had been sitting there on a bench in the park watching them for over an hour when a young lady walked up to me and said. Mr. Kane! Are you Mr. Ruben Kane?

I am I said and who are you.

My name is Martel, my father called you a few weeks ago and asked you for help but you never got back to him.

I remember I said. I was on another case and he was supposed to call me back but never did. My secretary lost his phone number, is he still needing help?

No Mr. Kane he's dead, he was murdered.

I'm sorry to hear that I said is there anything I can do?

There may be Mr. Kane, you can find the person or persons who killed him. If you're wondering about getting paid don't, I'll pay you the same amount my dad would have.

 I don't know Miss Martel as you can see I'm getting kind of up there in age and don't know if I can hack it anymore

my father told me that once a detective you always a detective, was my father wrong?

How old are you Miss Martel?

I'm 18 Mr. Kane, does that matter?

No, I guess not, you seem to know your mind.

Your father was a smart man,

 how can I help you?

Someone is stocking my mother, I think he's the same one that murdered my father.

And why would he be stocking your mother?

He's on old boyfriend of my mother's and he been fixated on her for years and I think he got tired of waiting for her.

Where is your mother now?

She's in hiding.

Have you call the police?

Only after my father was murdered, we told them all about the stocker. They been looking for him for the past two weeks but haven't found him. I think you would have found him.

I think Miss Martel your giving me too much credit.

The robber at the senior nursing home, the word is you caught him, and it didn't take you any time to do it. That's why I believe that you can catch my mother's stocker and my dad's murder, I know you can.

What about this stocker and what have the police said?

To be honest Mr. Kane, I think they're too busy with other things.

What do you know about this stocker? Do you have a name for me?

His name is Roger Banks and he's about 45 years old. 5 feet 11, about 220 pounds. Dark skin with a heavy mustache. He's all ways wearing dungarees and a western-style shirt, hat, and boots. He talks Texas.

He's not from this area then?

I don't think so Mr. Kane.

Any idea where I could find him?

No, I don't, but I hear he drinks a lot.

Does he have an automobile?

My mother thinks he has an Oldsmobile, blue. Texas license plates.

I'll tell you what miss Martel, I'll look around and see if I can come up with this Roger Banks but tell me this. What do you want me to do with him once I find him?

I hadn't thought that far ahead Mr. Kane, any ideas?

Thank on it for a while Miss Martel I'm open for suggestions, whatever you want; do you understand what I'm saying? If your father told you about me and my methods, then you understand what you're asking. Now let me ask you again, how would you like this handled?

I want you to get Mr. Banks off my mother's back and if he murdered my father I want him off permanently. Is that clear enough for you Mr. Kane?

Part 6

I stopped over at daddy Joe's barbecue grill to get me a dinner. Ribs, beans, coleslaw, and tea. I hadn't had that kind of food in a few weeks. I've forgotten how good food teats since eating at the palace. Don't know why they call it daddy Joe's, he's been dead now for 20 years or more, his son took over the place but he just as good as his dad. (Almost)

after eating I thought I needed a haircut but first I didn't want to run out of gas, so I stopped at the Mobil station.

$.18 a gallon I told the attendant, you guys trying to get rich?

Pretty soon you'll be looking at $.25 a gallon the attendant said.

When that happens, I'm getting me a bike I said. You goanna wash the windshield and check the tires for that price, aren't you?

Raymond's barbershop has been at the same location forever. E 79th and Cedar. He should be in his late 70s by now and I've been seeing him since in high school.

Raymond is about 250 pounds, 6'4 and has a goatee. I come here not only because he's a decent Barber, but he also knows the latest of what's happening all over town, and with me being a private eye he's helped me immensely over the years. (For a few bucks that is)

Raymond what's the latest? You looking good?

Don't lie to me Ruben I'm about on my last leg. Come on, get in this chair, you next.

I heard about that job you took care of at the senior home, they all praising you over there.

How do you know about that Raymond, nothing much gets by you does it?

Now, you know me Ruben, what can I help you with today? There is always something to bring you over this way.

There may be a little something Raymond that you can help me with.

A guy walking around in Western attire. Hat, shirt, pants, and Western boots. Go's by the name of Roger Banks, he may be driving a blue Oldsmobile.

Maybe, maybe not Ruben. How much is it worth to you?

I may be able to lay a twenty on you?

Make it twenty - five and it'll show come back to me.

I reached in my wallet and pulled out a twenty-dollar bill and a five. He started talking, I had a hard time getting him to stop. He started talking about stuff I never even asked him about. I'm glad I didn't have to pay him for all that, didn't think I had that much money in my wallet.

This guy in the cowhand duds, you can't miss him. I began noticing him a few weeks ago, it's not like you can miss him. He been hanging around with Rags, you remember him, don't you? The deadbeat. He will do anything for a dollar.

Has he been in here yet?

Not yet Ruben but I'm sure he will, everyone comes into Raymond's before it's over. You won't to tell me why you're looking for him?

A lost and found project for a young girl, looking to help her mother, I don't think there's nothing to it.

Knowing you Ruben, I know there won't be. I hope there won't be any killing this time, you seem to can't get away from the killings.

Now where did you hear that Raymond, I'm not a violent man, you know that.

Back at the office it seemed like I had just missed Rita, she left a note for me telling me my wife call and so did my girlfriend. Bernie called and said that I owe him $15.

I looked in my bottom desk drawer and there was a full bottle of Jack Black, I took it out and grab my coffee cup and poured a large hit, the night was still young, and I was debating where I should go next.

If this Roger person is a drinker, then I imagine I should hit the clubs. Ebony club, cave club, rainbow room, rooster tail club, or the standalone club. I forgot the one-night stand club and the Boomerang club (that's a gay club) no one said the man was gay but then one never knows.

Part 7

At 7 PM I went over to Hastings's pool hall to shoot a round or two, the place never changes. 10 to 12 tables and all full. I got in line at number six table and took me a sit-down at the shoe's shine chair. Ordered myself a beer and looked around the place. There were a few guys I knew, and I waved at them and they did the same. 20 minutes later a slot came open and I started playing. In the middle of the third set two men walked in one was wearing a cowboy hat. I was so distracted until I missed my next shot. One person in the room said Rags. Haven't seen you like forever. I've been around rack said. That Missed. shot made me lose the game plus $20. I watched Roger and Rags grab a beer and set on a bench and started talking to people they knew. I grabbed me a beer and took it outside to my car.

Two hours later they came out, got into the old's and drove to the rooster tail club. I followed them, they set at the far end of the bar and I set at the opposite end. A tall dark skin woman was sitting at one of the tables and started walking toward Roger and rags. Roger looked like he was surprised to see her, they talked for a few minutes and then she slapped him, more than once. Roger raised his fist and hammered her upside the head and she hit the floor. When she got up she stumbled back to her table, Roger ran out the bar and told rags to follow him. I watched the woman reach her table and her handbag. She bought out what looked like a 38 and brought it around to where Roger used to be. She looked toward the door and all there was the door swinging close. All the people at the bar was on the floor that included me. I got up and follow Roger and rags out the door and spotted them half a block down the street entering the old's. My Buick was a block in the opposite direction and I made for it. By the time I got turned around the old's was nowhere in sight

if I couldn't find Roger I thought I'd head back to the rooster tail. That same lady was sitting at the table with three other girls and they were trying to calm her down. I tried to get close enough, so I could hear what they were talking about.

One said, now Penny you know that wasn't right, you see the man don't want you so leave him alone. The girl named Penny said. No man is going to fuck over me like he did. I'm going to put one of these 38's up his ass and send him back to Texas. Another one of the girls at the table said. Penny you need to stop that. Another one of the girls said. We were having fun before you start that shit.

Fuck all you bitches, I'm getting the hell out of here.

You can't go anywhere bitch, I'm driving.

Fuck you bitches, Penny said, I'll take a cab.

Outside the club the last cab had just pulled out I was right behind penny, she started cursing and I asked her was it anything I could do?

No, she said unless you have a car.

I've got that I said. Where you want to go?

I'd like to go home she said. But I don't have anything to drink there. Do you know of a quiet place to get a drink?

I think I do, I said.

Who was that bitch, rags said? She really had it in for you?

Her name is Penny and she's been stalking me for over six months now, I guess I made it to good for her, how did I know she would get into me. Like that. Who knows the direction a batch is going to go? Anyway, in about the third or fourth month she started talking about getting rid of her old man. I thought she was talking about leaving him but no, she's talking about killing his ass. I had to tell her, no way was I killing anybody. Then she says, suppose I kill him would you go away with me then?

I thought she was just shiting me, so I say yes.

Two weeks later I see in the paper that he was dead. (That was in Houston you understand) and I got the hell out of Texas. I come to Ohio of all the states I could have come to, I come here.

She put the shit on me, even got her kid thinking I killed him. That's the third time I've run into her with the same outcome. Maybe Alaska. That should be far enough.

You think she would have shot you Roger?

Hell, yeah, and you do too, the way you were hanging on my coattail when we left the bar.

I don't think we should be hanging out together anymore Roger, she may miss you one night and hit me.

You joking aren't you rags, things not that bad.

I'm not kidding Roger that's one thing I don't do, and he finished his drink and walked out the door.

Damn, rags is the only friend I have in Cleveland maybe I should take my own advice and get the hell out of Ohio. He reaches for the phone and call the train station when is your next train to Alaska he asked?

Part 8

The cave club

was at a location on a dead end road that normally cater to live jazz music but since this was a Wednesday they had none.

The club was almost empty, and few people were there, all couples.

How did you find this place Penny asked?

By accident I said. It hasn't been here long. We sit at a table in a corner near the wall. The waiter came over and we ordered our drinks. gin and tonic for her and a Jack Black for me. Penny was quiet and didn't say very much and I let it go at that. Remembering the last time, I was there I was at that same table alone when I spotted a couple at another table that look like they were really into each other. Holding each other's hands and kissing and doing other things that I couldn't see. Reminded me of myself when I was younger. The two crossed arms and toasted each other and kissed again, got up and headed for the door. I followed them with my eyes, it was then that I realize that the woman was no other than my wife.

What are you thinking about penny asked.

Oh, just reminiscing, I said. Giving you a chance to settle down. Would you like another drink?

Yes, I would she said.

After the waiter had come and gone with their drinks I turned to her and said. Want to talk about it?

You don't want to hear about my troubles, if you're feeling bad now you're really be feeling bad after I tell you what I have to say. But to make a long story short-I was married living in Houston Texas, my husband was murdered. There after my daughter and I moved to Cleveland. There was a man involved and he promised to do something for me and didn't, I don't like that. When someone says they're going to do something for you they should do it.

That guy in the bar?

That was him Penny said.

Would you have shot him, I asked?

She just looked at me. Yes, she would have shot him, I thought. What's your name she asked me?

Ruben Kane, I said.

You are that PI my daughter contacted to find Roger?

Yeah, you could say that I said I see you found him. Let me tell you this Mr. Kane I decided tonight that I'm finish with this hate and payback with Roger, so you can stop looking for him. I'm leaving Ohio and leaving it to him.

We departed the cave club and I dropped her off at her apartment as she was getting out the car I asked her. You said you were leaving, anyplace special you were thinking about going?

Yes, Penny said. I've got my sights on "Alaska".

Part 9

Rita!

Has the mail come in yet?

Yeah R.K., it's under all that bullshit you have on your desk, or it may be in your trash can. You know you do that sometime after you come in loaded. Try there.

I got it, it was in the trash can.

Rita! Have you seen my coffee cup? You know that's the only cup I can drink my JB out of.

Look in the bathroom by the toilet or by the couch where you fall out nights after you come in..

I set back in my chair and poured a shot of JB, glanced out the window on the park and the street below. Going through the mail there were the water bill for the apartment with my wife, the gas bill, and the rent. I don't understand why I'm sent a bill for that it's only two dollars a month.

Now why I'm paying two dollars a month for on office building that would rent for many dollars more. A few years ago, I did a job for the banker who owns the building and gave me a lifetime rental for two dollars. Not a bad deal, I think. There were a few other junk mail items but the last one was from the state of Alaska but no name. I think I know who it was from because I knew only one person in Alaska and that was Smooth. It's been years since I've heard from him, he left Cleveland when they tried drafting him. He was pimping here in the city and had five or six girls working for him. He took them all with him and ended up in Alaska. The last letter I received from him says he's doing very well. But then he always did do good. He says that he has over twenty girls now.

R.K., the reason I'm writing you is that I ran into a woman named Penny, she said that she knew you.

 Check this out, we were sitting at the bar just shooting the shit and a person walked in and she saw him and went berserk. She reaches in her purse and pulled out a 38 special and before I could stop her she shot him five times. She's in jail right now for murder.

Well that's the bad news, maybe I'll have some good news for you the next time I write.

Take care

Yours truly

Smooth

End

Other books by this author:

Enlisted at 14…A Memoir

Enlisted at 14 and the journey continues

Enlisted at 14… Looking back

Willow… A novel

Willow… One for the team

Willow… And the Medusa

Little Miss Willow… A Short Story

Assassin

Blacker the Berry

Meet Ruben Kane

R.K. {Ruben Kane}

Ruben's bag

Ruben's bad side

Smooth…A Ruben Kane novel

Mo Kane

Here Tis'

and then some

dear client

Ducks in a row

Just a dream

Dream Catcher

Beyond the curve

first one in

Switch

Dumas…Outrageous

Well I'll be

Redemption

41

42